```
796.6      Glaser, Jason.
GLA           Snow mountain biking /
```

HILLTOP ELEM. LIBRARY
WEST UNITY, OHIO

HILLTOP ELEM. LIBRARY
WEST UNITY, OHIO

Snow Mountain Biking

by Jason Glaser

Content reviewed by:

International Mountain
Bicycling Association (IMBA)

CAPSTONE
HIGH/LOW BOOKS
an imprint of Capstone Press
Mankato, Minnesota

Capstone High/Low Books are published by Capstone Press
818 North Willow Street, Mankato, Minnesota 56001
http://www.capstone-press.com

Copyright © 1999 Capstone Press. All rights reserved.
No part of this book may be reproduced without written permission from the publisher. The publisher takes no responsibility for the use of any of the materials or methods described in this book, nor for the products thereof.
Printed in the United States of America.

Library of Congress Cataloging-in-Publication Data
Glaser, Jason.
  Snow mountain biking/by Jason Glaser.
  p. cm.—(Extreme sports)
  Includes bibliographical references (p. 44) and index.
  Summary: Describes the history, equipment, and contemporary practice of snow mountain biking.
  ISBN 0-7368-0169-3
  1. All terrain cycling. 2. Winter sports. [1. All terrain cycling. 2. Winter sports.] I. Title. II. Series.
GV1056.G53 1999
796.6'3—dc21
                                                                    98-45523
                                                                         CIP
                                                                          AC

Editorial Credits
Matt Doeden, editor; Timothy Halldin, cover designer; Sheri Gosewisch
   and Kimberly Danger, photo researchers

Photo Credits
Index Stock Imagery, 33
International Stock, 34–35; International Stock/Tony Demin, 15; Eric Sanford, 39;
 Caroline Wood, 40
Mary E. Messenger, 12
Photri-Microstock/Breton/Wallis, 8
The Picture Cube/David Lissy, 4, 36
Todd W. Patrick, cover, 7, 11, 16, 18, 20, 23, 24, 26, 29, 30, 47

Table of Contents

Chapter 1   Snow Mountain Biking 5

Chapter 2   History of Mountain Biking 9

Chapter 3   Competitions 19

Chapter 4   Equipment 27

Chapter 5   Safety 37

Features

Photo Diagram 34

Words to Know 42

To Learn More 44

Useful Addresses 45

Internet Sites 46

Index 48

Chapter 1
Snow Mountain Biking

Snow mountain biking is a sport in which people ride mountain bikes over snow and ice. Some snow mountain bikers race on snow and ice courses. Some racers compete in short, fast races called sprints. Others compete in long races that take days to complete.

Snow Mountain Bike Racers
Snow mountain bike racers do not all compete together in the same races. Men and women compete in snow mountain bike races in

Snow mountain bikers ride on snow and ice.

separate classes. Racing classes also may be based on age. Some races include men and women of many different ages.

Most snow mountain bike racers do not ride mountain bikes only on snow. They ride on other surfaces such as streets and dirt paths. But snow and ice surfaces add danger and excitement to mountain biking. Mountain bikers are more likely to crash on snow or ice than on other surfaces.

Speed

Mountain bikers can go faster on snow and ice than they can on other surfaces. Snow and ice provide less traction than other surfaces. Snow and ice do not slow down bicycle tires as much as normal ground does.

In 1996, Carolyn Curl set the record for bike speed on snow in Les Arcs, France. She rode her bike down a mountain at 115 miles (185 kilometers) per hour. Many snow mountain bike racers reach speeds of 75 miles (121 kilometers) per hour.

Racers may have trouble stopping or turning on slippery snow and ice surfaces.

Racing mountain bikes on snow and ice is dangerous. Racers can easily lose control of their mountain bikes. Racers may have trouble stopping or turning on slippery snow and ice surfaces. But most snow mountain bike racers enjoy the thrill and challenge of their sport.

Chapter 2
History of Mountain Biking

People began building mountain bikes in the 1970s. The first mountain bikes were a cross between 10-speed bikes and BMX bikes. This cross allowed people to ride 10-speed bikes on rough surfaces.

10-Speed Bikes

Early bicycles had only one gear. These bikes worked well for traveling over flat surfaces. But bikers had to pedal hard to travel uphill or against strong winds.

Mountain bikes combine features of 10-speed bikes and BMX bikes.

In the 1930s, an Italian inventor created a device called a derailleur (di-RAY-luhr). The derailleur allowed cyclists to shift the position of the bicycle chain to different gears. The derailleur and gears allowed bikers to change the force required to pedal. Bikers could pedal faster or slower depending on the terrain.

Bicycle manufacturers used the derailleur design to build bikes with many gears. The most common of these new bikes was the 10-speed. These bikes had 10 different gears. Some gears were good for travel on flat and smooth surfaces. Others worked better for traveling up or down hills. Bikers could shift gears while they rode.

BMX Bikes

Manufacturers began to build BMX bikes during the 1970s. People use these small, sturdy bikes to race on motocross courses. These short dirt courses have many dirt mounds that serve as jumps.

Mountain bikes have gear systems that allow cyclists to change the force required to pedal.

BMX bikes are durable. Cyclists can ride them over jumps and rough terrain. The bikes' small, strong frames and wide tires prevent damage to the bikes. But BMX bikes have only one gear. Riders cannot change gears for different riding conditions.

Early Mountain Bikes

Some bicyclists wanted to ride their 10-speed bikes over rough terrain such as dirt trails. But regular 10-speed bikes were not durable enough for this. Riders began modifying their 10-speed bikes. They made them more like BMX bikes. They built bikes with sturdier frames and wider tires. They called these new bikes "clunkers."

People also called clunkers "all-terrain bikes" or "mountain bikes." These bikes were strong and durable like BMX bikes. They had more than one gear like 10-speed bikes.

BMX bikes have strong frames and wide tires.

Mountain Bike Racing

Mountain bikes became popular during the 1980s. Bicycle manufacturing companies began making and selling the bikes. Bikers could ride mountain bikes on many kinds of terrain. The bikers did not need roads. Some people started calling this kind of bike riding "off-road biking."

Mountain bikers rode on trails with many obstacles, such as trees, rocks, and logs. Mountain trails were a popular place for mountain bikers to ride. Groups of mountain bikers gathered at mountain trails. The group members raced one another up and down the trails.

In 1983, a group of bikers formed the National Off-Road Bicycling Association (NORBA). This group set up races and made rules for mountain bike racing. NORBA is still an important group in the sport of mountain biking today.

Mountain bikes became popular during the 1980s.

Snow Mountain Bike Racing

The first organized snow mountain bike races were held in the late 1980s. But the sport did not gain wide popularity until the late 1990s. That was when it became a part of the X-Games. A television network called ESPN hosts this competition each year. Athletes at the X-Games compete in many different extreme sports.

Snow mountain biking first became part of the X-Games in 1997. People enjoyed watching the racers on the snow and ice courses. Bikers enjoyed the thrill of the competition.

Snow mountain bike racing became popular during the late 1990s.

Chapter 3
Competitions

There are three main kinds of snow mountain bike races. They are downhill, speed, and enduro races.

Downhill Races
Downhill races take place on ski slopes. These races also are called slalom races. Slalom race courses have many twists and turns. Bikers must avoid obstacles and go through sets of flags called gates.

Slalom competitors at the X-Games race two at a time. The bikers ride side by side.

Slalom races have many twists and turns.

Slalom racers must go through gates.

Judges time each biker's ride. Bikers switch sides after their first ride. Then they race again. The judges add each biker's two times. The racer with the fastest combined time wins the race.

Speed Events

Speed events take place on ski slopes with no twists or turns. Racers ride their bikes straight down the slopes. They pedal hard to gain as much speed as they can. Racers who go too fast often lose control of their bikes. This can lead to dangerous crashes.

Speed racers also race two at a time in speed events. They race down the slope twice. Then judges add each biker's two times. The biker with the fastest combined time wins the race.

Enduros

Enduros are long mountain bike races. Enduros get their name from the word "endurance." Endurance is the ability to do something for a long period of time. Enduro racers must travel many miles to reach the finish line. Some enduro races last up to one week.

Enduro racers must carry camping equipment, food, and tools on their bikes.

They need this equipment because the races can last several days. Racers often cook their meals over small campfires. They must fix their own bikes if they break.

Bikers who win enduro races must do more than ride fast. They must manage their time and equipment well. They must keep a steady pace over a long period of time.

Most enduro races take place in rural areas away from cities and towns. Racers often must cross long stretches of wilderness. Many snow mountain bike enduro races take place in Alaska and Canada. These places often have a great deal of snow and ice.

Iditasport

The most famous enduro race is the Iditabike. The Iditabike is a 100-mile (161-kilometer) race that begins near Anchorage, Alaska. It is part of a larger competition called the Iditasport. People may race in the Iditasport on bikes, skis, or snowshoes. Racers have 50 hours to finish the Iditasport.

Most enduros take place in rural areas.

The idea for the Iditasport came from the Iditarod. The Iditarod is a sled-dog race that began during the 1970s. In 1982, skiers created their own race similar to the Iditarod. They called this race the Iditaski. Soon, people on snowshoes and on foot joined the race. Race organizers added the Iditabike in 1987. All these races combine to form the Iditasport.

The Iditasport Extreme is a longer version of the Iditasport. Racers in this competition must complete a 320-mile (515-kilometer) course. Most Iditasport Extreme racers need about one week to finish the race.

Bikers often race for several days during enduros.

Chapter 4

Equipment

Mountain bikes have special features. These features allow them to travel over many kinds of terrain. Snow mountain bikers modify their mountain bikes for snow racing. These changes to regular mountain bikes are important to the bikers' safety on snow and ice.

Bikes

Mountain bikes must be strong and durable. Bumps on tough courses put strain on bikes. Mountain bike frames are built with light, strong metals such as aluminum and titanium. Mountain bike frames are thicker and stronger

Mountain bike frames must be strong and durable.

than regular bike frames. This prevents them from breaking easily.

Mountain bikes have suspension systems. Suspension systems absorb much of the impact of bumps. They allow bikes to go over bumps without being damaged.

Mountain bikes usually have straight handlebars. A brake lever is attached to each end of the handlebar. Bikers squeeze the levers to use their brakes. Each brake is connected to a wheel. One brake stops the front wheel. The other brake stops the back wheel.

Cables connect the brake levers to clamps called calipers. Calipers squeeze rubber pads against the wheels to stop them from turning.

Handlebars also have shifters. Bikers use shifters to change gears while riding.

Tires

Snow mountain bikers use wide tires that can grip snow and ice surfaces. Wide tires also keep bikes from sinking into the snow. Some

Mountain bikers control their brakes with levers mounted on the handlebars.

snow mountain bikers do not keep their tires completely full of air. Tires become flatter and wider as air is let out. Tires that are not completely full of air get better traction.

Most snow mountain bike tires have bumps and deep grooves called tread. Tires with deep tread grip surfaces better than tires with shallow tread. Some bikers add small metal studs to their tires for more traction. This additional traction is important because snow mountain bikers ride on slippery surfaces.

Some mountain bike racers use special tires called slicks. Slicks have no tread at all. Tread slows down bikes. Snow mountain bikers may use slicks for speed events. Racers in these events do not have to turn their bikes much. They do not need much traction. Usually only experienced bikers use slicks. Slicks make bikes difficult to control.

Enduro Equipment

Enduro racers must carry equipment on their bikes. They carry sleeping bags and tents to

Tread and metal studs help tires grip slippery surfaces.

keep them warm and sheltered at night. Racers also bring food. They often bring dried food because it is light. Enduro racers bring small pots to melt snow over fires for water.

Enduro races run through the day and night. Racers need flashlights or bike-mounted lights to see where they are going at night. These items also help others spot the racers.

Many enduro racers bring tools and extra tires. Enduro races can be hard on bikes. Racers must fix their bikes if they break.

Enduro racers often carry equipment in backpacks.

Handlebar

Brake Lever

Brake Cable

Frame

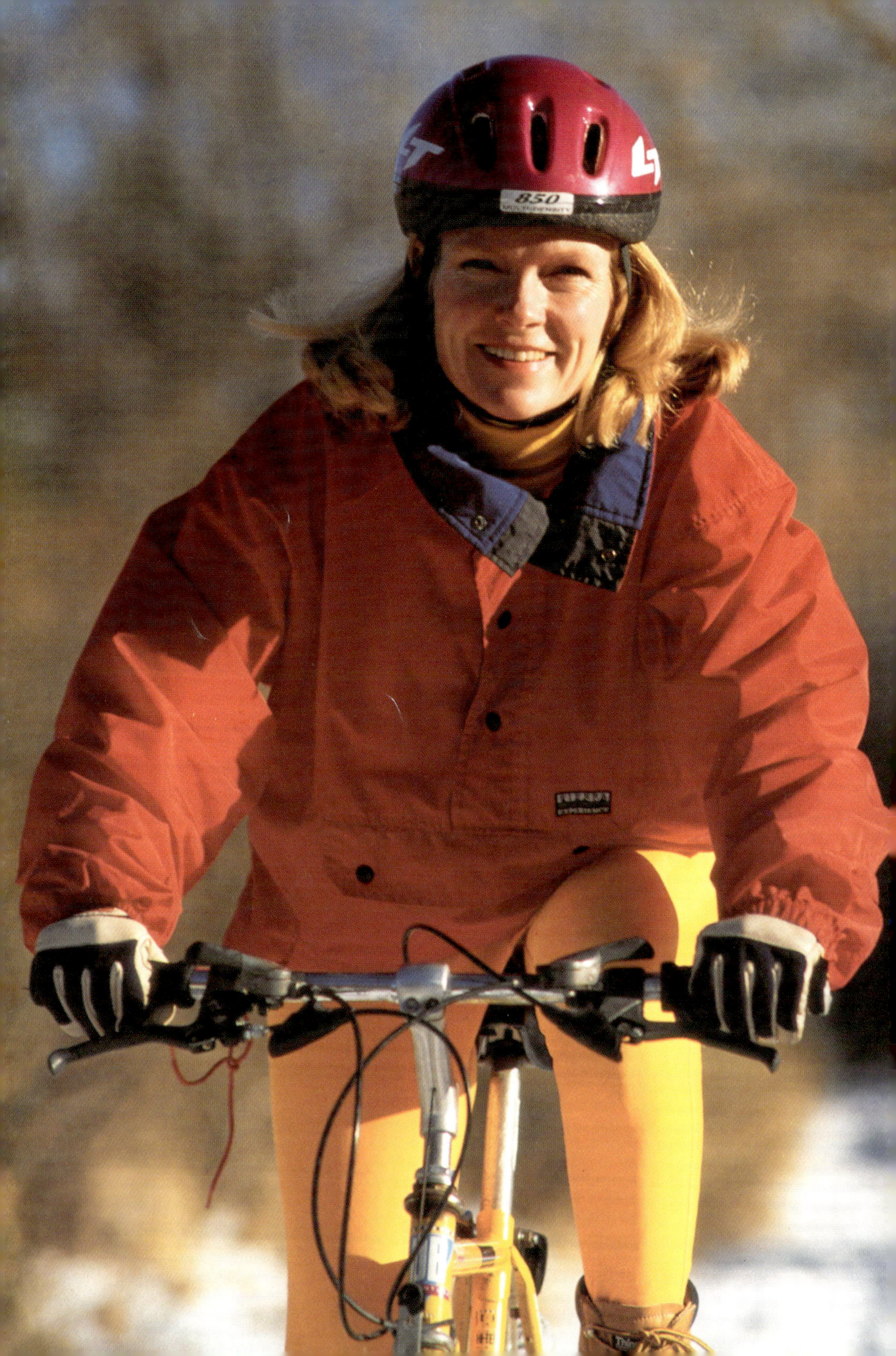
850

Chapter 5
Safety

Snow mountain bike racing is dangerous. Bikers travel at high speeds over slippery surfaces. Cold weather and winds add to the danger. Bikers take special measures to stay safe.

Clothing
Snow mountain bikers wear warm clothing and padding over their entire bodies. They wear many layers of clothing. The layers protect racers from the cold. They also protect racers from injuries during falls.

Snow mountain bikers wear helmets to protect their heads during crashes and falls.

Mountain bikers wear helmets to protect their heads during crashes and falls. Some racing helmets have face shields that protect bikers' eyes and noses from cold air. Other bikers wear goggles or glasses.

Gloves keep bikers' hands warm. Handlebar grips can become very cold. Gloves prevent damage to the skin from the cold air and handlebar grips. Some riders carry extra-large mittens called "pogies." They warm their hands in the pogies during breaks.

Bike Maintenance

Most snow mountain bikers maintain their own bikes. They make sure everything is working before riding. They check their bikes' brakes, chains, and tires. They also clean their bikes after riding. Keeping bikes clean helps keep them in good condition

Bikers must pay special attention to their gears and chains. These parts can stick easily in cold weather. Bikers use special grease to keep bike gears and chains working in the cold air.

Warm clothing helps to prevent hypothermia.

Cold and Snow

Snow mountain bikers face dangers from cold and snow. One danger is hypothermia. This condition occurs when a person's body temperature becomes too low. One way bikers avoid hypothermia is by eating well before riding. Eating well supplies bikers' bodies with extra energy to stay warm.

Racers must drink plenty of water.

Frostbite occurs when cold air freezes uncovered skin or skin next to wet clothing. Bikers can avoid frostbite by dressing warmly and covering all their skin.

Snowstorms can make objects hard to see. Riders may not be able to see obstacles. Car and truck drivers may not be able to see riders. Riders should have bike lights and reflectors so others can see them.

Rules of the Trail

The International Mountain Bicycling Association (IMBA) created a list of rules for all bikers to follow. It calls this list the "Rules of the Trail." This list tells riders to do six things to ride safely:
    1) Ride on open trails only.
    2) Do not ride on muddy surfaces and do not litter.
    3) Obey all speed limits.
    4) Be thoughtful of other trail users.
    5) Never scare or tease animals.
    6) Always plan ahead.

Other Safety Measures

Bikers must drink plenty of water during races. They will become dehydrated if they do not have enough water in their bodies. Bikers keep water bottles in holders on their bikes or wear backpacks that hold water pouches.

Snow mountain bikers should always ride in groups. Group members can help one another in case of problems. They also can share water or other equipment if needed. Group riding helps riders enjoy their sport safely.

Words to Know

aluminum (uh-LOO-mi-nuhm)—a light, silver-colored metal
calipers (KA-li-purs)—a set of clamps at the end of a brake cable; calipers press against a wheel to stop it from turning.
derailleur (di-RAY-luhr)—a device for shifting gears on a bicycle
durable (DUR-uh-buhl)—tough and lasting for a long time
endurance (en-DUR-uhnss)—the ability to do something for a long period of time
enduro (en-DUR-oh)—a long mountain bike race
frame (FRAYM)—the main body of a bike
frostbite (FRAWST-bite)—a condition that occurs when cold air freezes skin
hypothermia (hye-puh-THUR-mee-uh)—a condition in which a person's body temperature becomes too low

maintain (mayn-TAYN)—to keep in good working condition
modify (MOD-uh-fye)—to change to fit a specific purpose
obstacle (OB-stuh-kuhl)—an object that prevents normal travel
slalom (SLAH-luhm)—a race in which competitors must go though a set of gates
slick (SLIK)—a tire that has no tread
terrain (tuh-RAYN)—ground or land
titanium (tye-TAY-nee-uhm)—a light, strong, silver-colored metal
traction (TRAK-shuhn)—the ability of a moving body to grip a surface
tread (TRED)—a series of bumps and deep grooves on a tire; tread helps tires grip surfaces.

To Learn More

Allen, Bob. *Mountain Biking.* All Action. Minneapolis: Lerner, 1992.

Gutman, Bill. *Bicycling.* Action Sports. Minneapolis: Capstone Press, 1995.

Gutman, Bill. *Mountain Biking.* Action Sports. Minneapolis: Capstone Press, 1995.

Hautzig, David. *Pedal Power: How a Mountain Bike Is Made.* New York: Lodestar Books, 1996.

Useful Addresses

Canadian Mountain Biking Alliance (CMBA)
27 Cornerbrook Drive
Don Mills, ON M3A 1H5
Canada

Iditasport Information
11441 Browder Avenue
Anchorage, AK 99516-1237

International Mountain Bicycling Association (IMBA)
P.O. Box 7578
Boulder, CO 80306

National Off-Road Bicycling Association (NORBA)
1 Olympic Plaza
Colorado Springs, CO 80909-5775

Internet Sites

ESPN.com Extreme Sports
http://espnet.sportszone.com/extreme/index.html

Icebike
http://www.enteract.com/~icebike/Default.htm

Iditasport
http://www.iditasport.com

IMBA
http://www.imba.com

NORBA
http://www.usacycling.org/mtb

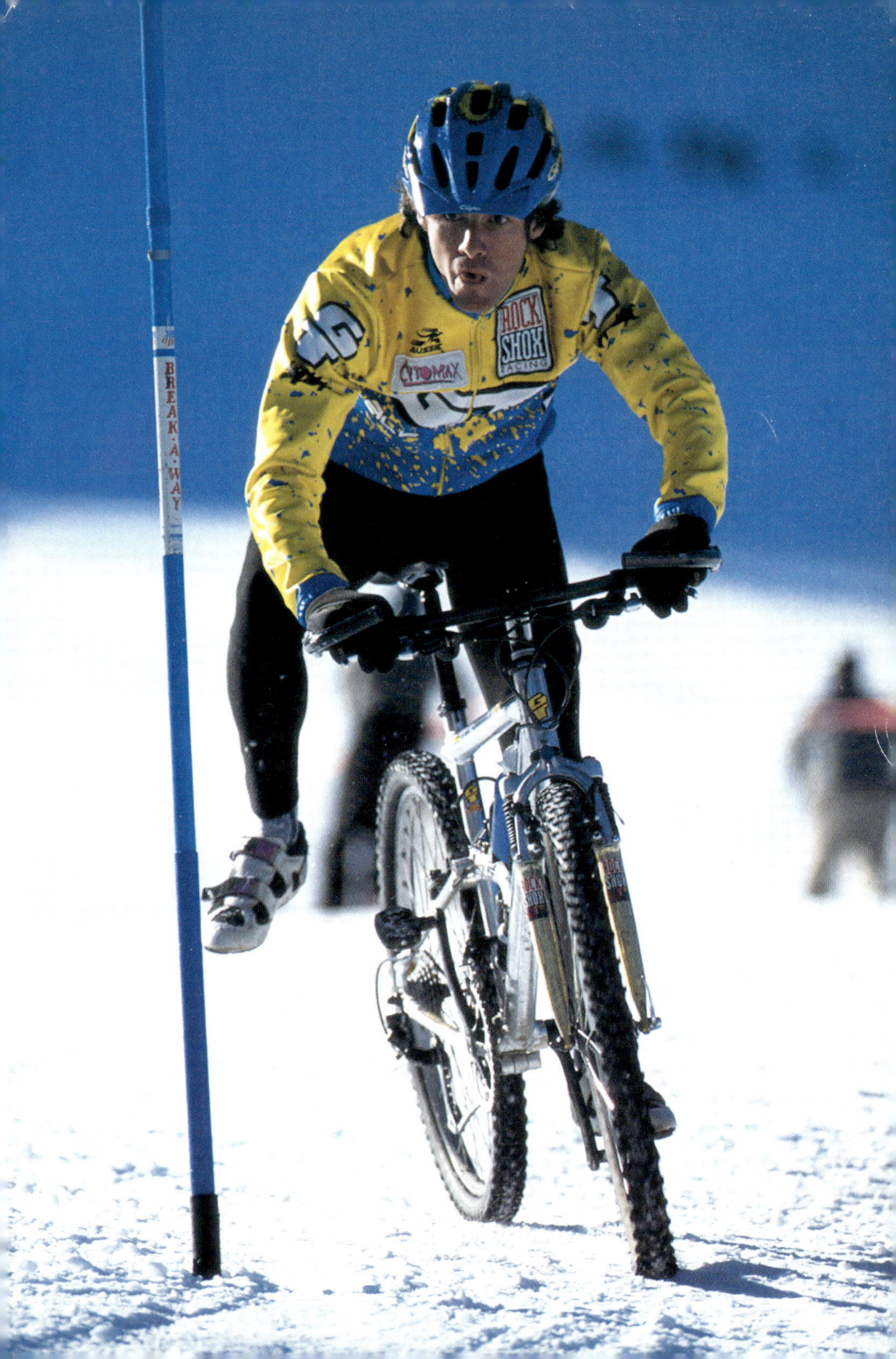
BREAK-A-WAY
ROCK SHOX RACING
CYTOMAX

Index

aluminum, 27

BMX bikes, 9, 10–13,
brakes, 28, 38

calipers, 28
chain, 10, 38
classes, 6
clunkers, 13
Curl, Carolyn, 6

derailleur, 10

enduro, 21–22, 31–32
ESPN, 17

frostbite, 40

gates, 19
gloves, 38
goggles, 38

helmets, 38
hypothermia, 39

Iditasport, 22–25

International Mountain Bicycling Association (IMBA), 41

National Off-Road Bicycling Association (NORBA), 14

obstacles, 14, 19, 40

pogies, 38

Rules of the Trail, 41

slalom races, 19–20
slicks, 31
speed events, 21
suspension systems, 28

10-speed bikes, 9–10, 13
titanium, 27
traction, 6, 31
trails, 13, 14, 41
tread, 31

X-Games, 17, 19